T0209304

DEADLY DESIRES

MICHAEL DAVIES

DEADLY DESIRES

iUniverse books may be ordered through booksellers or by contacting:

iUniverse
1663 Liberty Drive
Bloomington, IN 47403
www.iuniverse.com
844-349-9409

ISBN: 978-1-6632-4003-3 (sc)
ISBN: 978-1-6632-4004-0 (e)

Library of Congress Control Number: 2022909151

Print information available on the last page.

iUniverse rev. date: 06/14/2022

CONTENTS

1

BIRTH OF THE TITANS

Deep in the dark of night, amidst the wilderness of the provenance that would become Mexico City, screams of terror and pain echo through the black of night. Enraged mobocrats with torches lit, rope ready and armed with swords chase after a known rapist and murderer. Alerted to their advance, Athenas Hernandez peered behind him and watched for their arrival. With blood dripping from his fangs and running down his neck, he dropped his victim and turned to run.

But it was too late. The villagers had caught up and surrounded him. The hombres were tall and masculine. Muscles rippled their bodies from the hard labor of working the land. Judge Mendez pushed his way through the mob with his men, Martins and Philips and stood before him. Two musclemen held him while a third bound his hands. Philips proceeded to the victim's side. Kneeling on bended knee, he raised the victim's head and examined the wounds on her neck. "She's dead," he confirmed. Having carefully rested her head on the ground, he returned to the Judges side.

Athenas, "Pete," was a strikingly handsome man. Standing at six feet six inches, he towered over most of the citizens of the provenance. His muscular, Heman body was complete with large pecs and sexy pronounced six pack abs. His huge cut cock hung between his legs like a snake. His shoulder length hair flowed in the gentle breeze. His gorgeous face was edged by sideburns. His coco brown skin shimmered in the moon light. His lean, firm ass was the envy of some and the fantasy of others.

Mendez glared at Hernandez with disgust. "Kill him," he ordered. Nunez and D'Angelo forced him to a nearby bolder and held him down while Philips dug a crucifix from his pocket and fastened it around his neck. "Hahaha," Pete laughed while Griffon held the cross for him to see," You bastards think that will stop me? NO, Senors! I will return from the depths of hell, and I will reduce this city to burning heaps of rubble! NO ONE shall escape my wrath! I will wage war on all your generations to come! None shall be safe! I will rape your women and girls, and sodomize you men and boys, young and old, none shall escape me!"

"In the name of the Father, The Son and His Holy Spirit, I send thy soul back to HELL, Athenas Hernandez!" Pressing the crucifix to Pete's forehead, Griffon glared coldly at him while his flesh singed, blistered and smoked. "Aww," Athenas roared in his demonic voice," You fucking son of a bitch! I will hunt you and your seed to the ends of the earth for this!" Griffon ripped his shirt open and pressed the point of the stake to his hairy chest.

"All your generations shall know my face, feel the prick of my fangs and the pain of my pecker up their asses! I shall seduce them, male and female, and none shall be rid of me! And I shall feed on their blood forever, Griffon Philips!" "In the name of The Almighty, I send thee to HELL," Philips, yelled. Blood gushed from his body as he commenced to drive the stake into his body. "Aww," Pete called out in a demonic roar. Raising to strike the final blow, Griffon Yelled," Die you son of a bitch!" Pete spouted blood from his mouth one last time, that ran down his face.

Griffon drew his sword from its sheath and raised it to finish the job. "That will do, Philips," Mendez said. "If I do not decapitate him, he WILL rise from the grave." "I said, Enough! I don't believe in such foolish superstitions. Just throw him into the damn hole and be done with it!" "Yes, sir."

Athenas glared at him and growled through clenched teeth as he pulled the stake out. Grabbing Nunez and D'Angelo, he snapped their necks and they fell to the side. Catching Philips by the throat, he dug his claws deep into the flesh. "Aww," he cried out. A Mobocrat drew his sword and prepared to strike, but Athenas caught it by the blade, disarmed him and ran him through. Blood gushed from the man's mouth and gut. Philips ran up behind the beast and struck him over the head. With the help of another, he dragged his body over to the grave that had been hastily dug and threw him in. With the deed done, the mob disassembled and slowly abated, leaving the grave alone in the heart of the wooded area.

The moon radiated in the midnight sky and cast the solitary grave in a silvery light. With the stars twinkling within the heavenly expanse, a rumbling suddenly began. The earth and grave commenced to shake. The loose sand proceeded to erupt from beneath and soon a bloody claw broke through the soil. Pete emerged from the grave roaring long and loud while rising into the air. Flying through the sky, he began bombing the buildings with firebombs. Shooting waves of energy from his brow, he engulfed would be survivors in flames. Within seconds, the city lay in ruins, and the inhabitants were dead, all but one man, Griffon Phillips. They're bloody and blistered bodies polluted the landscape like the aftermath of a plague.

In the cold, dark depths of space, a ship settled beyond the reach of earth's gravitation. Cloaked from all instruments of detection, the secret deeds proceeding within its frame would silence the naysayers and confound the wise. Within the metallic walls of the lab, the necessary tools laid out, ready for use.

The laboratory itself was not uncommon to any one would find on earth and resembled a doctor's office. A metallic examination table complete with straps and a pad rested near the far wall, Xray machine hovered near the table with a cart for instruments off to the side. On the counter was a computer monitor and keyboard displaying pictures of the human sperm doner and the course of the egg, a vampire bat from earth.

Groan entered the room with his assistant, Gyro. Groan stood at seven feet three inches tall, Gyro stood at seven foot four. Both were sixty three but still well within their prime, and looked to be thirty two earth years. Their collar length hair, pubic and body hair was almost black green. Their smooth, humanoid skin was Kelly green. Their almond shaped, humanoid eyes where hypnotic and was a jade green. Their athletic humanoid bodies rivaled the sexiest of Greek gods', and put the best of them to shame. With large pecs, huge guns and ripped abs, blanketed in just the perfect amount of hair the sexiest of any gay "bear" could have. Their huge twelve inch long limp dicks with their six inch girths would mesmerize most humans and be the envy of others. Their tapering torsos, small hips and small, well firmed asses were irresistible.

While Gyro tapped some keys on the pad, Groan opened and pulled his pants down. He removed his smock and hung it on the coat stand near the door then returned to the computer screen where a clip of two earth men engaged in anal sex in missionary style appeared. Groan's dick immediately stiffened into a eighteen inch boner with a seven inch girth. He lubed it while Gyro pulled his pants down revealing his eighteen inch boner. As the gay pornographic video played, they both jerked off.

Breathing heavily from the pleasure, they sped their stroke while the climax neared its apex. Feeling the orgasm rapidly approaching, they doubled over, parted their lips and sped their stroke. "Awww," they both moaned. As the orgasm raced to the brink, they grabbed test tubes and pressed them to their tips. "Aw-haaaaaaaaa," they moaned speeding their stroke. With a loud outburst of satisfaction, they shot their ample loads into the tubes, then panted while catching their breath.

With a few clicks of the keys, the images on the monitor changed to a camp ground. Marcas De La Luna lay in his sleeping bag under the star filled heavens watching them twinkle. His hands were under his head, and legs crossed at the ankles. On each side of him were his friends and roommates Hector and Fredrico. All three young men in their mid thirties, and irresistibly handsome.

They were all Latinos, six feet six inches tall, had shoulder length hair, circular beards, muscular athletic bodies with large pecs, and ripped six pack abs. All three had small, sexy shaped asses, and huge cut dicks. They were nearly Greek gods. With a touch of a button Marc was encased in a shaft of light that seemed to appear from nowhere. They all sat up and shielded their eyes, from the brightness. "What the fuck, dude," Hector said. Instantly, Marc vanished and reappeared strapped down on the examination table in nothing but the boxer briefs he had been wearing.

Groan readied the flesh jack- like instrument by lubing it up while Gyro pulled Marc's underwear down and removed them from his body. "No. No," Marc protested," What the fuck are you doing? No!" Gyro commenced to work the specimen's dick into a boner. "No! Stop! What the fuck? Guys, I'm not gay." "Just relax, Marc," Gyro told him," this shouldn't take long." "You speak English? Ok. What the fuck are you doing?" "Were not going to hurt you, we just need a sample of your sperm," Gyro said. "what do you need my cum for?" "That is none of your concern." "Yeah? Well I say if you want something I can get at least a hundred bucks a pop for, you'd better tell me what I'm shooting off for." "An experiment, Mr. De La Luna, a new race of humanoids."

"What for?" "That's not your concern." "If you'd rather, Groan said," we could do things the unpleasant way." Holding a needle in one hand, he held the flesh jack in the other. "The flesh jack will be best," Marc determined and swallowed. Settling at his side, Groan slid the toy onto Marc's huge boner while his assistant caressed his chest and abs. "Oh, fuck! That's incredible! What makes it feel so intense?" "The lube," Gyro answered," but the stud will have this sensation naturally." "Could I take some of that lube back with me after all this? That's amazing. Fuck, that feels good," Marc exclaimed.

Fifteen minutes passed, and Marc was now in the thralls of extasy. His body writhed, his breath was short, and his moans were loud. "I'm close guys! Aww, fuck! I'm gonna cum!" Releasing his man cream into the toy, Marc called out. "Holy shit," he exclaimed," I need a fucking cigarette!"

While Groan proceeded to fertilize the bat egg with his, Gyro's and Marc's sperm, Gyro cleaned Marx's cock up and freed him from his confines. Marc proceeded with him to Groan's side and watched them set the infused egg under a microscope and watched it divide and grow through the screen. "Wow," Marc said," That's really developing fast!" "You are free to watch, Mr. De La Luna," Groan began," but please keep your comments to yourself." "Yes. Of course. Sorry."

While a translucent leathery shell formed around the egg, the embryo took form. Groan Removed the specimen from the dish, and set it on the floor where it proceeded to grow and develop at a phenomenal rate. Within seconds, the hybrid was the full size of a nine month old human baby. A claw poked through the elastic like membrane and punctured a hole. Watching the baby slice an incision the length of the cocoon like shell, it fought and struggled to get free. Poking his head through, he took his first breath. Gyro picked the infant up and nursed him with a bottle. Hearing his cries of pain as they circumcised him, Marc covered his dick and winced in full sympathy. "That's not pleasant," he said.

As they dressed the wound, Marc stood at Gyro's side. "What are you gonna name him." He asked. Groan met his inquisitive eyes. "After you," he informed. "Is that satisfactory," Gyro asked. "Yes. That's fine." Having burped the babe, Gyro laid him on the table where he grew to the age of puberty in seconds. The lad glanced around the room taking in his surroundings as he proceeded to grow to adulthood, or the equivalent of 18 earth years. He linked eyes with Gyro. "What is this place?" His father, Marcas sat next to him and put his arm around him. "Don't be afraid," he told him," I won't let them hurt you."

With a wave of Gyro's hand, Marc the doner vanished. Marc peered into his eyes while he settled in front of him with a tagging gun. "What happened?" "He's alright. He's back where he came from," he explained. Having pressed the gun against Marc's shoulder, he pulled the trigger. The instant sting of the chip being shot into his shoulder was nearly unbearable. "Ow," he cried out as blood trickled down his arm. The wound instantly healed without any sign of injury. Groan settled next to him with a loin cloth in his hand. "Put this on and come with us."

They led him into a room with a long wooden table in the center with padded chairs set around it. A large screen spanned the width of the west wall and was 65 inches tall. With the stroke of a few keys, a presentation played on the screen about the Inter Galactic Genetic Research Program, and its purpose. Marc learned that he was merely one of millions like him created to seduce, romance and mate with humans on earth, making them unwitting subjects in this tactic to gradually take over the world. The gender of his targets was irrelevant, though he had been intended to prey upon the male population. Genetically engineered to ejaculate an egg as a fifth emission at every orgasm. Therefore, he was genetically programmed to be attracted to human males.

At the end of the film, they turned their chairs towards him. "Do you have any questions," Groan asked. "Am I a good person, or bad?" "You have to decide that for yourself," Gyro told him. "The favorable range of age of your targets are anywhere from 11 years to 45. But anyone under the age of 18 is considered an adolescent and are protected by the law. However, age is unimportant. A host body is a host, age is irrelevant," Groan explained. "We recommend, you don't get personally involved with your subjects," Gyro said," Do the deed, shoot your load and move on. The more you can impregnate, the better." "How are the babies born? Who takes care of them?" "Like you, they grow to adulthood within a few minutes. They don't need anyone to take care of them or raise them," Groan explained. "If a stud is not present at birth, then the birth process will terminate the life of the host." "But how does it come out?" "Through the abdomen," Gyro continued. "Is there any way to prevent this slaughter?"

"They're worthless pieces of shit, Marc. Their pathetic lives mean nothing! They spend their time fucking, eating, sleeping, shitting and pissing. With their destructive natures they're destroying they're planet which is rightfully ours! We were here before their ancestors could even come down from the trees," Groan informed him. "We're a proud, noble race," Gyro said, "If it were not for us, these insignificant pieces of shit would have never become what they are today and the world would be a hell of a better place because of the Draconians!"

"Draconians? You're...." "Hybrids," Groan said," Only difference between you and I is our green hair and skin."

"Other than that, you can't tell the difference." "My god! But My skins..." "Like theirs," Gyro concluded, "Yes." "You're the perfect predator for carrying out your mission," Groan said. "Predator?" He looked up at Groan. "I am no predator! Neither will I be a part of this!" "No one is saying you're bad," he told him," You're projecting that onto yourself." Marc rose to his feet. "This has to stop," Marc concluded.

Having found his way to the bridge, he saw two guards stationed outside the door. He observed that they were more draconian than humanoid. He stopped in is tracks when he spotted them and pressed his back against the wall attempting to avoid discovery. He closed his eyes and concentrated to achieve invisibility. Succeeding, he proceeded openly down the hall. He drew the ray gun from one's holster and fired, striking both between the eyes. Their backs slammed against the wall and slid down as their lives ebbed to an end. The holes in their heads burned with flames and the stench of searing flesh permeated the air.

Facing the door head on, Marc blasted the control pad and kicked it down. Storming the bridge, he shot the two ensigns as they rose at their posts, advanced to the first and second officers blowing holes in their foreheads and striking them between their eyes. Their heads exploded like melons. The Captain rose from his seat, turned and fired at him but missed. The flare like ball of energy passing just a half an inch from Marc's head. Marc raised his gun and aimed it at the captain's head. "Lights out asshole," he said. He pulled the trigger, but the hammer clicked, nothing happened. The captain laughed, his long lizard tongue hung out the side of his mouth like a dog. With his draconian humanoid form scantily covered, his huge boner bulging in his tight pants, he raised his ray gun. "Times up asshole! You lose!" He pulled the trigger and the hammer clicked.

Peering at the gun the Captain growled in frustration. Marc caused a sword to appear in his hand and swung at him. He instantly drew his sword and blocked his blow. "So you wanna play, pussy? I'll play," Captain Mar said, then took a swing which Marc intercepted then jabbed. Mar turned to the side avoiding contact and laughed. It was clear he was enjoying the battle. He raised his eyebrows and cocked his head as he responded verbally. "Haha! You missed." Catching Marc of guard, he stabbed him, stepping close to him he held his face inches from his own. "But now, you're fucked," he continued and kissed his lips. With their lips centimeters apart, he stared him in the eyes and shoved the sword through Marcs abs. Blood poured out of his mouth and ran down his chin. Withdrawing his blade, the body fell to the floor.

Mar Proceeded to his first mate and examined his wounds. The wound in Marc's abdomen quickly healed with no trace of injury. The Captain waved his hand and the First officer's body and gore vanished. While he proceeded to and crouched next to his second officers side, Marc's finger twitched. While Mar waved his hand to clean the bridge of the remains of his lifeless mate, Marc sat up and put his hand to his groggy head. After a moment it had cleared. Mar cleared the bridge of his second ensign's body and blood. Sensing a presence, he turned and beheld Marc with red glowing eyes, showing his fangs he roared and sunk them deep into his neck quickly draining his body of blood and fluid, turning him into a dehydrated corpse. Marc withdrew his fangs and banished the remains to the outer limits of nothingness.

He turned to the two frightened Greys that stood in terror at the helm. As he slowly made his way to their sides, they trembled. They were about average height and were covered by smoke black thin strapped thongs with pouches holding their junk. Their large insect like eyes blinked and tears ran down their faces while he settled threateningly close to them. "Don't be afraid," he told them in their language," I won't hurt you. But if you want to live, I suggest you get off this ship." "We're slave master," one told him," We have nowhere to go or means to get there." "Set the self destruct mechanism on this ship and I'll send you back to your home." With a few strokes of the keys, the greys pulled up the grid to set the process in motion. They entered the commands and the button for activating the timer and count down was uncovered.

Marc waved his hand and sent them back to their planet and kind. Having pressed the button, he turned as Groan and Gyro entered with ray guns in their hands and two Nine foot naked Draconians with guns cocked. "We won't allow you to do this, Marc," he said," Surrender yourself and come with us, all will be forgotten." "I will not allow you to do this to the human race," Marc determined. "You don't understand. This is for their own good," Groan said. "Right! Complete extermination of their species is for their own good," Marc said with disbelief. "Not all of them will be eradicated, many of them will be assimilated become part of us. We're not gonna just irradicate them, Marc. That's why you were created to mix their DNA with ours and save their future generations," Gyro explained. "One," the moderated female voice said. Marc vanished just as a fireball swept through the bridge. The entire ship exploded into millions of fragments that sped to earth and decimated the country sides they struck and exploded like comets.

Reduced to a flaming sphere of dust and debris at the core of the remains, the existence of the ship was revealed and showed up on radar. "Uh, Sir, you need to look at this." "What is that," the general asked. "I don't know, but it's just outside earth's atmosphere." "All unites to your battle station pronto we got a bogie repeat, we got a bogie."

2

THE BLACK PHALLAS

It was a cold, dark autumn night in October, the week of Halloween when Ace Cruz slowly made his way along the walk of Main Street bound for a destination that would prove his annihilation. There wasn't a cloud in the sky. The moon cast its silvery rays on the small town below and transformed it into a mysterious world of dark shadows and dim light. The lifeless street seemed abandoned and void of inhabitants. The shops decorated for the dark holiday, seemed empty, and depraved of all activity.

The crisp, night air gave birth to the sight of the youth's breath which billowed like plumes of smoke expelled from the fiery nostrils of a dragon. The fallen, autumn leaves splashed in the colors of fall, crunched loudly beneath his feet and shattered the silence of night.

Ace was sixteen, not yet out of High School, but he was out on the prowl, looking to get laid. Turning the collar up of his shiny black jacket, he shivered in the cold. His shoulder length hair blew in the ice-cold breeze. His circular beard added to his sex appeal but failed to mask his true age.

His tight, black shirt was spread open to his sternum to display his large pecs. His boyish, nearly hairless body was ornamented with gold nipping rings in both tits. A masculine gold chain necklace hung from his neck. Dangling, gold earrings hung from each lobe completing the set. The fit of his tight, black, glossy slacks contoured to every form of his body revealing plainly his large dick, balls, and small sexy ass in back.

Having entered the foreboding realms of the lounge, he paused near the door and absorbed the ambiance of this forbidden abode, unaware of the certain danger that awaited. Finding it common to any other bar one might enter, he discovered the form of entertainment this drab hangout afforded to its tenants through the posters and signs hung on the walls and the equipment he beheld. It sported a dance floor, karaoke post and a few gaming machines with darts. In the other room were two billiard tables set end to end with tables and chairs along the wall posed for spectators.

There were less than a dozen guys presently seated along the counter. For reasons unknown, there were no women in attendance. Ace concluded that it must be a hangout for guys only. Most were in couples and groups of threes and fours, while one or two sat alone. All the tables were vacant and free for the taking. A tall, strikingly handsome Latino stood behind the counter tending bar.

Mesmerized by Athenas, Ace locked eyes on this studly wet dream and iconic fantasy. Having an insatiable appetite for sex Pete loved playing the field and was a notorious playboy.

Tending bar allowed him to meet a parade of various guys on a personal one on one basis and cater to his animalistic drive for a new partner every night.

He had abandoned his thirst for revenge on the generations of the inhabitants of New Mexico decades ago, but detected their lineage by the scent of their blood. He had gained better gratification in fucking their asses and draining them of their life force. Catching the scent of Aces blood, he instantly knew he descended from, Martins.

Ace swooned at Pete's "Tall dark and handsome" appeal. His perfect, long hair rippled to his shoulders and glistened under the dim lights of the pub. His hairy, athletic body with large pecs and six pack abs was unavoidably on open display. The cup of his black thong did little to contain his nine inch, cut cock, bulging within and left his sexy, well firmed ass exposed for all to see. He appeared to be about twenty eight years old.

Turning to his rear, he met Ace's wonton eyes. With lust building between them like mercery rising in a barometer, he smiled in his usual seductive manner and they commenced to stroke at their stiffening dicks. Exchanging "What's up" nods, he approached him. "What'll it be, sexy," he asked. Ace peered at Pete's huge, thick cock peeking through the sides of his cup. A lust filled grin brightened his expressions as he met his eyes. "Miller.... And uh... your huge cock up my ass," he flirted and licked his lips suggestively.

"Hahaha. How old are you?" "You don't wanna fuck me, stud?" "How old?" "Twenty one." "Haha. Bull - fucking – shit! Let's see your ID." Digging his wallet from the confines of his back pocket, he tossed his card on the counter. Having taken a look, Pete tossed it back. Taking a glass, he threw some ice in and filled it from the tab. Setting it before the boy, he placed his arms on the counter and peered into his gentle brown eyes. "Three bucks," he announced. Ace drew the cash from his wallet before returning it to his pocket. He held the money out between two fingers. "Here's a five. Keep the change," he said, smiled then gave him a wink.

Taking a sip, he turned away in search of a place to sit. "Why don't you sit up here," Pete suggested, "Or ain't you got the balls to hangout with the big boys?" Proceeding to open his pants, he responded. "Oh, I got balls… BIG… balls. Wanna see'em?" "Hahaha. Keep your pants on kid." "I got balls bigger than yours, I'll bet," He challenged. Athenas laughed and gave him a nod. "You want a pissing match, boy? Anytime, anyplace." A sexy grin brightened his smug expressions. Taking another sip, he slipped onto a nearby stool. Guzzling down a healthy amount of beer, he let out a loud belch.

"Como te llamas, guapo? What's your name?" "Ace." "Hahaha. Ace?" "You got a problem with that, capullo?" "Kinda sissy name. Ain't it?" "Fuck you! I was named after my grandfather, asshole! He gave his fucking life for the freedoms you now enjoy! So try to show some fucking respect!" "Alright! Alright! Ya got a big cock, Ace?" He grinned then laughed devilishly. "The biggest you've ever seen, putada!" "Hahaha. How old are you really?" "Old enough," He said with a flirtatious grin. Resting his arms on the counter he leaned in and continued seductively. "Old enough for a sexy stud like you to fuck my tight…little ass."

Uncovering his twelve inch long boner, Pete allowed him to check him out. "Anytime you think you're man enough to take this fucking beast up your skinny twink ass you just let me know." Studying his sexy body and huge hard on, Ace chewed on the end of his straw with a lustful grin. Pete covered his dick while the twink rose to his feet and took a few steps towards the men's room. Pausing, he peered over his shoulder back at him with an inviting, sexy smile. "Come on, Stud," he lured, "Time to mount up cowboy." "Hahaha. Oh, HELL yeah, baby!"

Joining his side, he placed his hand on the boy's small ass and pressed his lips to his ear. "I'm gonna fuck your ass so hard you won't be able to sit for a week!" "Hahaha. Yeah? I'm gonna ride your massive cock so hard you'll beg for mercy!" "Aw, fuck yeah, chico!"

The men's room was skanky, like in a bathhouse with precious little appeal. The walls were bare and drab, a metal sheet finished the west wall near the urinal. A solitary sink provided the washing of one's hands. A single urinal that didn't flush was separated from the toilet by a wall without a door. There was no mirror.

Having bolted the door, he took the boy into his arms, licked him from his neck to his tongue and kissed his open mouth heavily. With passion feverishly raging within their senses, he ripped the youth's shirt open and removed it from his body. It vanished before reaching the floor. He commenced to flood his neck, pecs and abs with wet sensual kisses. The boy parted his lips and tilted his head back drawing in the pleasure that dominated his senses. Athenas caressed and groped at the boys back, legs and ass like a rabid beast. With insurmountable pleasure coursing through their emotions, their breath became heavy, moans proceeded to escape their lips.

With unfathomable pleasure coursing through their veins like a freight train speeding uncontrollably down the track, Pete opened the twink's pants, pulled them down revealing his small, sexy ass. His pants and white legless briefs disappeared without a single thought as he continued his groping and pawing at the boy's body, fueling their passions and consuming their senses. Pete lifted Ace's leg and wrapped it around his waist.

Pressing his glans, or tip to the kid's asshole, lube appeared on his giant cock. Pulling his boner back like a snake preparing to strike, he violently swung him around, pushed him forward and took hold of his hips. Catching himself on the sink, Ace cringed and moaned, writhing as he felt it slowly go deep inside him. With gasps of bereavement, it was nearly more than the boy could bear. "Aww! Fuck! Fuck, me! Aww, dude," Ace cried out.

Driven by a primal animalistic force, Pete fucked his tight ass long and hard, taking him to heights of ecstasy he never knew existed. For fifteen grueling minutes he pounded and ravaged the boy's body and pillaged his senses. Just as they were both about to shoot off, he plunged his fangs into his jugular and proceeded to slowly drain his body of blood and fluid. Feeling the sudden sting of his fangs he cried out and panted. "Aww," Ace responded.

Within seconds, Ace's youth gradually drained from his features and he slowly withered into an old man as his voice mutated to a deep, eerie groan. Never breaking his stride, Pete tensed up, threw his head back, cried out and increased his speed while he fucked Ace's lifeless, brittle corpse. Nearing the orgasm, he fucked him like some demon from hell in heat.

His eyes glowed red, as he roared, "Aw fuck! Shit! Aw My God! That's good!"

While shooting his cum into the dehydrated old vessel, he continued to call out loudly. Oozing from the dried remains, his cum lubed his massive boner. "Fuck! Fuck! Oh, Fuck! Yeah! Yeaaah! Hu! Hu! Shiiiit! Fuuuuuck! Yeaaaaah! Ho! Fuck! That felt good! Damn! You're a good fuck, kid!"

Pausing, he took a moment to catch his breath. After pulling his massive cock from the fragile body, he pulled his thong up. Taking A moment to gaze at the brittle corps, he gave it a shove. Striking the concrete floor, it shattered like a porcelain doll. Adjusting his dick in his cup, he stared at the face which had broken off from the body which laid in broken fragments.

The once handsome youth had become the wrinkled discards of an old man. Stripped of his youth and essence that afforded him the worship and lust of the masses, he now lay forgotten, rejected and repulsive to a generation and society obsessed with the young and beautiful. Stepping through these shards to the door, the crunching of pottery breaking the silence of the moment, Pete paused, looked back and with a simple wave of his hand the mess vanished, banished to the exiles of nothingness without a trace of the boy's existence. Returning to his post behind the counter, he resumed his duties and conversation with the same customer as before. The passing of time forced the ebbing of darkness. With the dawn of morning came the first light of day dispelling the murderous deeds of Athenas Hernandez.

Ashton Philips, fifty six, lay fast asleep in his bed when his twink roommate of twenty four ripped a long loud raunchy fart, while asleep in his bed against the opposite wall. Waking to the toxic cloud of fumes, Ash gagged. Sitting up he threw his pillow at him. Jade Cruz, who often went by "Stone," woke and sat up just in time to catch it. "Fucking A, dude," Ash exclaimed," What the hell have you been eating?"

Putting the light on, Stone threw the blankets back revealing his huge boner. Following his old roommate into the bathroom, he paused with arms folder, legs crossed at the ankles, and shoulder leaned against the frame. Watching Ash proceed to the toilet, bare his three incher and commence to piss, he scratched his balls and stroked his long cut dick. Entering after Ashton flushed, he moved to the sink. While the old man washed his hands, he stroked his cock a moment longer before proceeding to piss.

He chuckled when he saw Ashton try to sneak a peek. Having set the plug, Ash pulled his black boxer briefs down, exposing his small, firm ass, and observed him standing at the toilet jerking off, his nine inch dick boned up to twelve inches. "Damn, dude," Ashton protested," Don't do that shit while I'm in here! Fuck!" "What the hell are you pissing about? I see you do it all the time!" "I'd appreciate it if you didn't do that while I'm in here." "Why not? Does it turn you on, or something? You want me to fuck you Ash?" "NO! Of course not! Damn! You watch me jerk off!" "Every chance I get." "Why?" He shrugged. "I like it." "You like to watch me stroke my tiny boner?" "Yeah. And it ain't that small." "Thought you were straight." "I am. I just like watching you beat off. I'd join ya if I had the time."

Glancing at him stroking his boner, Ashton, turned away. "Would you stop that," Ash demanded. "Fuck off!" "Jade!

Come on dude! Please!" "Don't bullshit me, Ash! We both know you like it! Oh, fuck that feels good!" "Do that in your bedroom!" "No! Oh! I'm close!" Jade increased his speed and writhed forward as ecstasy seized his senses. "Oh, yeah! Oh, FUCK!" Mesmerized by his self pleasure, Ashton turned to him face on and watched him. Stone turned his body to him, and commenced to fuck his hand, sliding his dick back and forth with his hips.

"This turn you on? Huh? You want this?" Peering at his small boner at full mast he chuckled as Ash swallowed. "Yeah ya do." Ash swallowed nervously, wondering what the hell had gotten into him. While Ashton turned to the sink, Jade stepped close to him and sped his stroking. "Aw, fuck," he said," I'm real close now dude. I'm gonna squirt any minute now." "Well, don't spray it on me!" "Oh, fuck! Awww! Dude! Aww! Aww! I'm gonna cum! I'm gonna squirt it!" While calling out with each emission, he shot his sperm onto Ashtons abs, chin and mouth.

Jade laughed as Ash wiped the cum from his lips and licked them. He then glared at him. "Thanks a lot, asshole!" "Hahaha! Hey! How's it taste, Ash?" he stroked at his boner as he continued. "You want some more?" "Fuck off you asshole!"

"Oh, Shit! I sprayed you good," he continued as he peered at the cum running down his roommate's face. "Hahaha! Like that, don't you?" "What makes you think I would even remotely enjoy something like that?" "Cause you're gay, faggots like weird shit like that. Especially when straight guys do it. It's like they yearn for someone they know they can't have, or some kinda shit like that." "Well, I'm not like that. And the next time you do that, I'm gonna cut your damn pecker off!"

"Hahaha! Sure, you will! You ever try, and I'll shove my giant cock straight up your bony ass!" "Don't try and bullshit me! You'd never get that thing even close to my ass! And you'd certainly never fuck me."

Jade had graduated from college that spring, but meeting some difficulty getting started in life and meeting Ashton in a gay bar decided to move in with him after getting to know him better over a few drinks. Ash was always a weird one though, never drinking alcohol even while in a bar. He got his number and moved in with the senior after texting.

Stone was a handsome young stud who liked guys, but wasn't gay. In his words, "I like fucking ass, don't care what gender it comes with." He was a Greek God-like hunk with ebony skin and irresistibly gorgeous features. Standing at six foot six with broad shoulders, small hips, tapering athletic hairy ripped body, he was primed for all sports and had a super hero appeal. His nine inch cut dick made him the envy of thousands and the wet dream of millions. His small, sexy shaped, firm ass turned on all who saw it.

Ashton stood at five foot five, had collar length fading blonde hair, wore no facial hair, had a lean, virtually hairless body riddled with several scars and a small cock. His Yellowish teeth were crooked. His often, unshaven face seemed to take on a youthfulness of ten years his actual age. His, nerdy, boy next door appeal had been tarnished with the passage of time and stripped him of desirability from the masses.

Within the National Guard Recruiting Center, the conversation ebbed to a close, Ashton sat in the General's office opposite him with the desk between them. Rising to their feet, Ash extended his hand in a gesture of comradery.

"Thank you for your time, General," he said. Grasping hands, they cordially shook. "I'm sorry to have to turn you down, sir," was Wilson's response, "You seem eager to serve your country." "I understand the rules, sir."

Advancing to the door he turned as General Wilson reached out for it. With his chest touching the back of his shoulder and their faces inches apart, Ashton felt a sudden wave of emotion and desire to kiss him. The expression on the general's face indicated that he felt the same inclination. After the intimate moment swelled to its apex, Wilson slowly moved in for the joining of their lips. Ashton turned his head and opened the door. "Thanks again, for your time, General," he said.

Taking his chin, he turned his face back to his and kissed him. With a deep seeded yearning to be loved imprisoning his emotions and reasoning, he relented. The general kissed him a second time, deeper and with more feeling than the first. Ash moan and pulled away. The handsome general still in his prime took him into his arms, kissed him deeply and with passion filled vigor. Placing his lips to his he spoke with a deep gentle voice. "I'm lonely too, Ashton. I need someone to love just as you need someone to love you. You're a bottom. Aren't you?" "Yes," he breathed. "Good. That's good. You have my number baby. Don't be a stranger." Giving him a deep, passion filled kiss, he caressed his ass and thigh. Absorbing the tidal wave of affection that flowed from his seductive touch, Ashton automatically succumbed by caressing his back and ass.

With their faces pressed together, the General beheld two younger soldiers advancing their way. Peering into his tear filled eyes, he released Ashton and took a step back. Passing through the door, he felt the General's hand on his ass. Wilson watched him enter the head, while the soldiers joined his side. "That him," Marisco Sanchez asked. "Yes. You know what to do." "Yes sir," Marco De La Luna replied.

Approaching one of the three urinals, Ashton opened his pants. Settling in place he exposed his dick and proceeded to piss. The two soldiers caught his attention as they entered. Immediately, he stopped pissing and stood there uncertain what he should do. As if restricted by some unseen force, he watched them in fear, unable to look away, as they advanced towards him unzipping their pants and digging their huge, unusually long snake like cocks out through their flies. Settling at the urinals on each side of him, he swallowed nervously and watched them closely through his peripheral.

They looked normal enough, stunningly handsome, but there was something about them that just wasn't right. Their cocks, though cut appeared somewhat common, but extremely long and thick, fourteen inches long with a seven inch girth, limp. He didn't want to know how big those beasts were boned up. Swallowing nervously, and trembling uncontrollably, he observed them openly look at his three incher. Hearing their piss colliding with the water in the urinals, and them moaning as they ogled his body, he stood there fighting to move. All he could do is close his eyes and pray for deliverance. Desperately attempting to make his body work, he soon discovered the ability to initiate his retreat. He quickly put his dick away, closed his pants, and made a hasty exit. The two watched him, vanished and poised to intercept him.

Reappearing outside the building, they waited with arms folded, legs crossed at the feet and their shoulders leaned against the doorframe. Ashton, abruptly stopped as they cut him off when he emerged from the Center. "Excuse me, gentlemen," he said while brushing Marc's body. Feeling their equipment meet sent a wave of desire through his senses, he gasped. "Sorry," he quickly muttered. "No problem," Marc answered watching him advance a few steps, "Hey." He stopped and turned to them. "Where are you headed?" "Job hunting." "Want a ride?"

Aroused by the raw, animalistic sex appeal these two studs exuded, and his attraction to their super model good looks, panic stirred within like the turbulence of the sea. "N-no... thanks." "You afraid of us Ashton," Marc asked inquisitively. Shocked that he knew his name without introduction, a frown briefly creased his brow. "Your mama taught you not to talk to strangers as a boy, huh?" Standing there a bit taken back, he found it impossible to respond. "My name is Marc De La Luna. This is my good friend, Marisco. You see? You can talk to me now that we've met." "I," he squeaked, "guess she must have." "You needn't fear us, Ashton," Marc continued," We're your friends. We're not gonna hurt you." His gentle, deep voice soothed his fears and pierced him to his soul.

Though they could read every thought and sensed every feeling he had, they kept this fact from him. "How old are you," Ash enquired. "What does that matter," Marc questioned. "I'm sure I'm old enough to be your granddad." "We're older than we look, but age is just a number." "So I've been told," Ashton said with deep thought. "Oh?" "I'd better, go. I got a lot of walking to do. It was nice meeting you." "We'd be happy to take you anywhere you need to go," Marc offered. "I can't afford to pay you." "Did either of us say anything about

money?" "I know I'm too old for you to wanna rape me....so....
what else is there in it for you?" "How about the satisfaction of
your company, Ashton?" Peering at them with an expression of
disbelief and suspicion, he paused, wondering what to think.
"It was nice meeting you guys. Thanks anyways."

Watching him walk away, they undressed him with their
eyes. "What do you think," Marc asked. "He'd make a fine
specimen," Marisco admitted," But he's clearly too old for
the project." "What if we changed him? Made him ideal for
what is wanted?" "Mhm. Maybe then." "I've never been so
sexually drawn to a human before! His cravings for love are
overwhelming! The aroma of his blood is almost more than I
can resist!" "So, fuck his ass and drink his blood." "He is more
than that to me, Marisco." "Weren't you cautioned not to get
attached to your victims?" "His soul cries out for love, I can't
just turn a deaf ear to his pleas."

"Were not here to rescue them from loneliness, Marc,
but to fuck their asses, plant our seed and move on. That's
our mission. I suggest you stick to it." "He yearns for me."
"Then give him your cock and leave him with your seed."
"No. There's gotta be something special about him or Wilson
wouldn't have alerted him to us." "Marc, buddy. I'm your best
friend. I don't want to see you get hurt. For all our sakes, stick
to the mission," Mirisco pleaded.

Standing at his post, Jade was closed to his girlfriend,
Chame Rodriguez of twenty one. They stood dressed in their
waitering outfits awaiting customer's arrival. Chame was a
beautiful Latina with long dark hair that past her shoulder
blades in back and churned like waves on the turbulent sea.
Standing at 5 foot 5, she was slender with huge boobs she often

put on display as one of her physical attributes. Her hour glass shape was subtle and allured the men to her like magnets. With a little eyeliner, mascara, blush and lipstick, she was the iconic vision of womanhood. Jade strove not to ogle her in her uniform avoiding an obvious hard on every time he looked her over.

"Damn Girl," he protested turning to her and observing her boobs nearly falling out of her top," Put those away! You're making me hard woman!" "You don't wanna see them, don't look," she replied. "Don't look? I can't help it! Come On, baby! Help me out here!" "Nu-uh! You don't like it, you don't have to look! I got a nice body and I refuse to hide it in shame!" "Baby, come on... I can't go around all the customers with a stiffy in my pants!" "That ain't my problem! If you weren't such a horn dog, you wouldn't get a boner all the time!" "Come on, baby. I'm dying here."

"Try thinking of something other than my big boobs and tight wet pussy for a change. How's Ashton?" "I practically boned his ass this morning." She gave him a look. "Excuse me? You did what?" "I almost fucked his ass." "Damn baby! You starting to bat for the other team?" "NO! Fuck, no, baby! It's just that he's so desperate and needing love. But you know I could never do something like that. "Mmhm. Well, he ain't in need of your big dick! Something that size aint meant to go up his ass but in my pussy! Fuck knows what damage your huge cock would do to him," Chame warned him. "He's like a bro to me baby," Jade told her tenderly. "Maybe we could help him. I have a couple of gay friends who're looking for a man. We could hook them up." "What would you do if I ever did fuck his ass?" "Ha! I'd drop kick your fucking ass out the door so fast your head would spin! I don't go for that shit!"

Continuing his job search, Ashton arrived at the next destination on his mental list and he entered the dimly lit world of the Dark Phallas. Taking a moment to scan the darkened domain, he observed that it was nearly empty. The usual crowd haunted the facilities in the common groups along the counter, behind which stood the bartender and owner, Athenas.

Catching the delectable sent of his highly fortified blood permeating the room, every head turned and every set of eyes searched to discover from whence it came. Repulsed by the age of the vessel of the source, the savory, aromatic fragrance soured in the senses of all. Complete rejection ensued and every inhabitant turned a cold shoulder.

Having given Athenas the once over, Ashton proceeded to an opening between the patrons at the counter and waited patiently for him to finish visiting with a favored customer. Shocked to see his bare ass and sexy, nearly naked body so vagrantly exposed and flaunted in public he looked down and stared at the counter top for a moment and swallowed nervously. Helpless against the barrage of imagery from glancing at his body, and the flood of emotion raging within, he felt his cock harden and gratification swell within his dick. Peering at Pete's sexy shaped ass, a sudden climax ravished his senses, an orgasm intensified and a small squirt messed his front while a moan escaped his lips.

Hearing his cry and sensing his accident, Athenas turned to him with an amused grin. Looking him over and detecting him to be a descendant of Griffon Phillips, his smile quickly abated and a sneer darkened his reception. Beholding his sexy, hairy, athletic body in a full frontal, Ashton gasped and proceeded to pant sharply. "Holy, shit," he breathed under his breath," It can't be!" Athenas settled in front of him, sickened by the fact that this old man was lusting after him and cuming himself in some erotic fantasy he had of him. "What do you want," he demanded. "Do you have any openings?" "You got any experience tending bar or waiting tables?" "No. But I can learn." "Then why waste my fucking time," he interrupted. "What about cleaning? I'll do anything." "Anything? Hahaha. Who'd wanna fuck a shriveled up old ass like yours?" Ash lowered his head in shame. "That's not what I meant," he muttered in defense.

Undaunted, he looked up and met his cold dark eyes. "Could I speak to the manager?" "I AM the manager, you stupid fuck!" "I see. Ok. Do you serve Pepsi?" "Coke!" "How much?" Seeing his persistence matched that of his ancestor, he stiffened his back and glared spitefully at him. "For you? Four bucks!"

Sensing a presence, Ashton turned and peered up into the eyes of the new arrival settling behind him. The tall handsome man was no stranger. With desire brewing within his senses, Ash began trembling. Smiling warmly at him, Marc held his gaze. How are you doing, Ashton?" "I'm good," he muttered.

Reaching for a napkin, he touched Ash with his shoulder. Feeling his muscular soft pec pressed against the back of his shoulder, the warmth of his body and with their faces inches apart, a spark ignited his desire for him and enflamed his passions and a gasp escaped his lips. Turning his face to him, their lips centimeters apart, Ash proceeded to breathe heavily.

"You alright," Marc asked. "S-sorry," he muttered. Swallowing nervously, he closed his eyes briefly to regain control. Turning his attention to Athenas, he continued. "Is the manager here?" "You're fucking talking to him, ya stupid ass! I just told you that!"

Ashton lowered his head in shame and sorrow. "I'm sorry to have wasted your time," he said sadly. Marc glared at Pete with anger while the "old man" headed for the door. "Was that really necessary?" "I don't wanna see his fucking old ass in here again!" "You're such an asshole!" Athenas glared at him and gave him the finger. Marc shook his head at him in disbelief of his ignorance.

Turning to the wounded soul, he vanished, reappearing at the door ahead of him. Intercepting Ashton, he pushed the door shut when he'd tried to open it. "Don't go," he gently pleaded. Peering up at him through a veil of tears, he sniffed and stated his defense. "I'm not wanted here." Taking his hand, he kissed it tenderly while gazing into his eyes. "Come sit with me," he invited in a loving tone.

3

TRANSFORMATION

Observing their every move, Pete seethed with hate as Marc took Ashton's hand and led him to a table. Moving a chair close, he sat next to him. Keenly interested, Athenas listened intently to what they said. Draping an arm across his shoulders, he peered deeply into Ashton's soft blue eyes. After a moment, he brushed a tear from his face before starting his inquiry.

"Tell me your name," he requested in a gentle, masculine deep voice. "Ashton." "You can call me Marc. How old are you, Ashton?" Breaking his gaze, he looked down in shame. "Fifty six," he muttered. Taking his chin, Marc turned his head back to him. Their eyes reconnected with his hand gently touching his face. "That's alright," he told him," That is nothing to be ashamed of. Age is just a number." With tears flooding his eyes, Ash gazed at Pete momentarily. "Not everyone believes that." "Don't let him get to you, Ashton. Did you just come out recently?" "No. Three years ago, when my mom died." "Been looking for a man to love you ever since?" "Yes."

"Where is your dad?" "Step dad," he promptly corrected," At this time of night, he's downstairs at home watching his TV." "You live with him?" "Not any more. I live with my friend now." "Does your step dad know you're gay?" "Yes. Since I was a boy." "Does it bother him?" "He doesn't give a shit! He's never cared about me!" "You may be surprised. You hate it here in Cedar Falls," he led," Can't wait to get out of Idaho altogether." "There's nothing here for me. No real culture, gay or otherwise! Everything is dominated by religionists, and no one wants to hire an old man like me, a good hard worker, NO! They want these young handsome bucks who do NOTHING but stand around all day bullshitting them and the customers! What little opportunity there is, goes to the college kids! I don't stand a chance in this damned one horse town! So... yeah. I hate it here!"

"Is your step dad your only family?" "I have an aunt and uncle here both on my mom's side. They care, but judge me for who and what I am." "Are you dominant, submissive, or versatile?" "Submissive. Only." "I'm dominant." Placing his hand on the back of Ashton's neck, he gazed seductively into his eyes and spoke in a deep, masculine voice that pierced him to his soul and gnawed at his heart with desire. "I will take you to heights you've never been before, and make you feel things no one else can. I AM your 'Mr. Right,' I AM your 'Fantasy man,' I will be your 'husband.' You've been looking for him a long time now. Haven't you?" "Yes," he breathed completely under his spell. "Any luck?" Swallowing nervously, he tried to answer. "The," he squeaked. Clearing his throat, he continued. "The bartender looks a lot like him," he paused and swallowed," So do you. The problem is, he hates me."

"I don't hate you, Ashton," he clarified. The sudden sound of Pete's voice startled him and he jumped at his abrupt appearance. "No? But I disgust you." Meeting his cold, dark eyes, he peered into them momentarily. Breaking the gaze, Pete turned his attention to Marc and held his gaze. "You wanna fuck his shriveled, old ass, be my guest. But don't pretend to be better or any different than me or anyone else here. I know who and…. WHAT you really are, asshole!"

Straightening in his chair and withdrawing his arm from across Ashton's shoulder he refused to back down or cower like a pup in some dark corner. "I don't know what you're talking about." Pete chuckled knowing he was fully aware of what he was hinting at. "And as far as my 'Fucking' Ashton's ass, that's none of your business." Placing his hands flat on the table and leaning in, Pete stared him back in the eye. "You fuck it in MY bar, and you make it my business, ass wipe!" Marc straightened in his chair. Glaring back at him, never breaking his stare. "Is there something you want, Pete," he challenged. He smiled, laughed devilishly and shook his head marveling at his perception. "Yeah," he admitted.

Breaking their intense gaze, he locked eyes with his intended victim. "I'm Athenas, Hernandez," he announced with an extended hand. "Ashton Philips," was his cordial reply accepting his truce with a friendly handshake. Raising his hand to his lips, he kissed it tenderly. The softness of his warm lips sent a tidal wave of desire through his senses. Swallowing nervously, Ash parted his lips and commenced to breath erratically.

While stroking his hand, Athenas continued his seduction and to spin his web of deception and drew him in one step at a time. "I'm sorry for the way I treated you before, Ashton," he repented," I hope you will forgive me." "It's alright." "No. It's not. I am sorry I hurt you. It's not usually in my nature to discriminate." "Let's just let it go. Please." "Yes. Alright."

Perceiving what Pete was up to, Marc took Ashton's hand. Steeling his attention, he peered into his eyes while giving his hand a tender kiss. "I have to go, baby," he told him," There's something I must attend to." Pete chuckled at his bullshit line. "I'd feel better knowing you were safe at home. Could I drive you?" "Yes," Ashton accepted.

Grabbing his arm, Pete dug his claws deep into his flesh. While Ash cried out, he glared into Marc's eyes. "He's staying with me!" Directing his attention to Ashton, Athenas turned to him and glared into his weak eyes. "Please…stay," he insisted. Wincing from the pain, he pushed at his arm for relief. With blood running down his arm and dripping from his hand, Ash bit his lower lip to withstand the pain.

The sight and scent of his blood nearly made Marc's mouth water. Going down on bended knee, he took his wrist and commenced to suck blood from the wound. Athenas, laughed. While Marc Fed, the wound healed without a trace. The blood inexplicably vanished and Marc commenced to lick and kiss Ashton's neck. Ending in a kiss, he peered into his eyes, took him by the back of the head, and kissed him with open mouth. Ash moaned with pleasure, barely able to withstand the severity of his passion. Knowing exactly what he was doing by this sudden outburst of affection, Pete glared at them. Ashton swallowed the mixture of their saliva and moaned as Marc proceeded to kiss and lick his neck. Giving him a third kiss, he peered into his eyes panting like a wild animal devouring his prey. "I want you baby!" "Too bad you have somewhere to go," Pete reminded.

"I will come to you soon, my love. We'll continue this then," Marc promised. Pete chuckled in his devilish manner. Accepting his plans, Ashton nodded. "I'll be waiting," was his response. Marc gave him another deeply passionate wet kiss, gently tugging his lower lip at the end. Ash swallowed, reopened his eyes and gazed back ready to be taken to the next level. Pete took him by the hand, pulled him away and took him into his arms. He watched Marc proceed to the door, pause, then disappear. He chuckled to himself. "That fucking son of a bitch wants to play games? I'll fucking play with him mono y fucking mono!"

Returning his attention to Ashton and drinking in his puppy dog look, as if he were begging him to fuck his ass, he continued to gouge his emotions. "How well do you know Marc," he asked. "I don't, really. We just met." "So, the fact that he just wants to fuck your ass doesn't bother you?" Taking a moment to think it over, he swallowed, then met his eyes. "I don't know. Maybe." "So… If I wanted to FUCK, your ass…. You'd be alright with that?" Knowing he was playing with fire, Ash swallowed and feeling trapped, thought he had no other choice but to play the game this devil seemed to be playing.

The thought of any man actually touching him in that manner both terrified and aroused his deep seeded need for a man to make love to him even more. Though Marc had ripped his heart open and left it to bleed by his sudden departure, Ashton's breath became short and erratic. "I-I… need to be loved," he defended. With beads of sweat rolling down his body, Ash swallowed nervously and trembled. Pressing their bodies together, Pete nestled his neck, and face. Kissing the side of Ashton's lips, he pressed their cheeks together and spoke gently into his ear. "Mhm. Well, you have no fucking idea of the world of SHIT you've just stepped into, Ashton! You want someone to fuck your ass, old man? I'll fuck ya! I'll fuck your ass so long and hard you won't be able to sit for a week!" After nibbling his lobe, he sucked on it. Feeling him nestle and kiss his neck, Ashton parted his lips and commenced to pant for air and moan in ecstasy.

Taking him into his arms, Pete Pressed their bodies together. Proceeding to caress and grope the back of his thighs and ass, he forced his tongue into his mouth and kissed him, ravaging his emotions and causing his dick to harden. With passion sparking between them like bolts of electricity, Ashton automatically relented to his seduction. Working his way down his face and neck, he showered his victim in wet kisses. "Ho-oh, man," Ash moaned while falling deep into his power.

In a heartbeat, they were both completely naked. Ashton was positioned on the table with his legs back and wide open. He saw Pete's twelve inch long boner wet with thick lube. Feeling his hands on his abs and the tip of his dick pressed firmly against his anus, he held his breath and tensed up with anticipation. Seeing Athenas for the demon he was, with horns and a deeply ridged red face, Ashton gasped and returned to his senses. "No," he breathed.

Struck with the overwhelming blow of pleasure of penetration, they both called out. Ash doubled over, holding his breath for as long as he could, and panted erratically as he felt him force his huge cock deeper and deeper till it was all the way inside him. "Stop," Ash cried, "Aww! Hu! Hu! Hu!" "Aww, fuck! Aww shit, you're tight," Pete growled in his demonic voice. Taking him by the hips he commenced to bang him hard and fast. "Aww," Ashton called out. "You like that, old man?" "Yes!" "Huh?" "Yes! Love it?" "Like my huge cock inside your ass?" "Aw! Yes!" Increasing his stride, Pete banged him harder. Ashton struggled but couldn't break free.

Feeling the pleasure raging within his senses, Ash fought to maintain control. Blood poured around Pete's huge boner and dripped from his balls as he fucked Ashton's ass hard. Ash drew his leg back and kicked him in the stomach as hard as he could. "Aw! Son of a bitch," Pete roared. He pulled his dick out but spun him around and shoved it back in and proceeded to fuck him from behind. "Get off me you son of a bitch," Ashton yelled. "Your little ass is mine old man!"

Having gone through a transformation during the assault, Ashton now appeared to be thirty years younger. The scars on his body and the skin graft on his right arm were gone, and the areas had returned to normal. His teeth were straight and bright white. No hair grew on his face or neck. Having grown to shoulder length, his hair had turned light blonde. His body was still lean and still virtually hairless. He was no taller than before, his dick was no bigger, but he was young again, and had a firm, sexy, small ass.

Ashton grabbed the beer bottle left on the table and broke it over Athenas' head. He grabbed his clothes and commenced to dress while Pete shook off the attack. "You little bastard," he roared and grabbed him by the throat. Ashton grabbed at his wrist as he tightened his grip and pushed at his arm. "You wanna play rough?" Throwing him across the room, Ash slammed into the opposite wall. Pete raced to him, pulled him to his feet by the neck and glared into his eyes. "Had enough? Huh? You ganna give in?" Ashton grabbed his wrist with both hands and kneed him in the balls. Having his briefs on he quickly put his pants on grabbed the rest of his clothes and left. With his bare feet slapping against the cold concrete he ran as fast as he could for as long as he could. Bracing himself against a building, he fought to catch his breath and commenced to finish dressing.

Having wandered passed Shoshone Street, The Depot Grill, and a few other businesses, he came to a large building with an open door. He proceeded up the front stoop to the door and entered. Turning right, he entered a dance room. Advancing to the left was a bar, straight ahead where some stairs which led to the restrooms. Stairs leading to a lower level remained unexplored by our curious adventurer. Descending the stairs, he met a tall exceedingly handsome man peering up at him. "May I help you," the stranger asked.

"I'm sorry if I'm intruding. The door was open, so I came in," Ash explained. Settling in front of this stud of a man, he peered up into his brown eyes. "What can I do for you," the man asked. "I'm Ashton Philips," he said with an extended hand. "Devlin Mendez, Owner and operator." "It's a pleasure to meet you." "El placer es mio, amigo mio." "I'm sorry.... I don't....." "Hahaha. It's alright. I'm just messing with you. The pleasure is mine, my friend." Ashton chuckled with relief. "Good. I was a bit worried for a minute there." "Hahaha. Just fucking with you, hombre."

Devlin gave him an inquisitive look. "What's up? You just in here checking things out or what?" "I'm actually looking for work, but I doubt I could do anything here." "Yeah? Can I ask you something personal?" "Yeah." "You gay?" "is it that obvious?" "You have that look amigo." "Great! Just what I need! Yes. I'm ...gay." "Ever do any drag before?" Ashton blushed. "No. A male version of me is bad enough." "I think you'd make one hell of a beautiful woman. I got an eye for these things." "I'd probably look something like my mom." "Then she must have been one hell of a good looking lady!"

"I still can't picture it." "You trust me?" "You've given me no reason not to." "You top, bottom or what?" "Bottom." "Mhm. I figured you were. You like men with huge cocks?" Ashton blushed and chuckled. "Yeah." Devlin unzipped and dug his giant dick out. "You like that?" "OMG! Is that real?" "Every inch. Like it?" "Yeah." "You mind that it's black?" "Not at all. They're my favorite." "Really?" "Yeah." "You like that it's cut?" "Yes." "You want it inside you?" Peering down, Ash turned away and chuckled while blushing. "I don't know." After a moment, he met his gaze. "Maybe," Ash responded. "Come with me."

Leading him downstairs, he took him into a sex room that was currently empty. With the lights on, Ashton could see all the spilled cum caked on the floor and shot onto the walls. He saw a wrestling mat in the middle of the floor with multiple cum stains and piles on its surface. Turning his attention back to his guide, he observed that he had opened his shirt and was now removing it. He noticed his huge pecs and rippling six pack abs and marveled at the massive amount of hair on both. "Come on, baby. Strip," Devlin invited. "I'd better be going," Ash said sheepishly, but watched as he opened his pants and pull them down revealing his huge 12 inch cock hanging between his muscular legs. Dev stepped close to him and proceeded to unbutton Ashton's shirt. Ash commenced to breathe heavily. He knew he should run, but he was drawn to Devin, he yearned to feel his touch. Removing Ash's shirt, Dev let it fall to the floor. Looking him over, Devlin then stroked his chest and abs. "Nice body baby."

Ashton gasped and writhed his body as Dev ran his hand from his chest to his navel. "You alright," Devlin asked. "Yes," he answered breathlessly. Proceeding to open his pants and pulling them and his boxer briefs down he took hold of Ashton's stiffening three incher and commenced to stroke it. His dick instantly hardened into a boner in his hand. Pulling away, Ash pulled his underwear and pants up. "I really should be going," he said. "Why are you fighting me, baby? Didn't you want the job?" "I don't think I'm right for it." Taking his huge boner in his hand he continued his seduction. "You don't want this?" "I…. do….but…." "You're afraid," Devlin finished for him. He took him into his arms and nestled his face. "I ain't gonna hurt you baby. I'll make it feel good." "I can't," Ash said with a gasp," I'm sorry." "Follow me."

Having dressed, Ash followed him into the office and waited for him to close the door. "What size are your briefs?" "Small." Dev crouched at a box in the closet and pulled out a few black thongs with rhinestone studs along the front strap, top and edges of the cup. "Your shirt size?" "Small." Devlin pulled four black vests from the closet. "See if these will fit."

Ash opened the package and slipped the thong on pulling at the strap riding up his ass. He then donned a vest and put the cap on. "Presioso," Devlin exclaimed," beautiful! Come. Let me make the final touch." Handing him a studded collar matching his thong, he settled behind the desk. "Come here." Settling before him, Ashton put the collar on then succumbed to his will. After lining his eyes with eyeliner, he added a little eye shadow and a natural-colored lipstick. "Perfecto! Muy sexy!"

Ash peered into the mirror setting on the desk and shook his head. "I look like a sex worker." "I think you look hot!" "I have to get home now," Ash told him." "I need you here an hour before you are to go on so Tony can show you what you need to do," Dev instructed. "I really don't know about this," Ash doubted, "Isn't there something else I can do?" "I need another dancer, baby. I'll try to find someone else, work you in where I can, but till then you're going on." "What time?" "Be here by 6 tonight. You'll work till closing."

Once home, Ash stood in front of the mirror of the medicine cabinet touching his youthful looking face with amazement. Removing the biker's cap and setting it on the sink, he examined his chest exposed by the open vest. Slowly running his fingers from his breast to his navel, he discovered he had pecs again and a slight six pack. While he removed his vest and set it next to the cap, his roommate entered. Settling at the toilet, Jade bared his nine incher and proceeded to piss while watching Ash. Having glanced at his large, cut cock, Ash marveled at the changes to his body. "OMG," he exclaimed under his breath," What have they done to me?"

Studying his features, Jade realized who he was and laughed. "Fucking A, dude! That's YOU? Hahaha! Holy shit! You're looking HOT Dude! What happened to your face?!" "What do you mean?" "I don't know, you just look different. Younger somehow. Love the makeup." "It's a long story."

"Hahaha. I was about to throw your ass out! But I had to piss like a fucking race horse, man," Stone explained. Peering back at him from the toilet bare ass naked, Jade glanced at his ass in the reflection. "Love the dog collar, bitch! VERY SEXY! Grrrr!"

Stone flushed and turned to him. With his hands on his hips, he watched him remove his thong and set it on the sink. Absorbing the thrill of Ashton's naked body, he stared at his three inch cock and joined his side. As Stone stood inches behind him, he peered down at his bare ass and drank in the sexiness of its small form. Wrapping his arms around his middle, he held his face inches from his roomy's and gazed at him through the mirror. "Mmm! Nice ass, baby!" Ash gazed back at him with bewilderment.

"Where have you been, sexy?" Feeling the intensity of the moment, and falling uncontrollably into his affection, Ashton commenced to breathe heavily. Covering his hardening dick, he sought to hide it from him. "Looking for a job," he said breathlessly then gasped. Stone nestled his cheek seductively and nibbled on his lobe. "Where did you get the outfit?" Releasing a brief moan, he stepped to the side attempting to fight his advances. Knowing he was breaking him down, Jade grinned devilishly, pulled him tight and pressed the tip of his huge boner into his crack.

"A guy gave it to me. Stone, don't!" Laughing devilishly, Jade nibbled on Ashton's lobe. "Yeah," he asked gently into his ear," Did he fuck you?" With his face to Ashton's, he commenced to grind his ass. "Hu," he moaned," Stop it Stone!" "Don't fight it baby! I know you fucking love it!" Pulling away, he stood in a side profile. "Just leave me alone!" Stone chuckled and slapped his ass. "You want me to leave you alone? I say bullshit! You think I'm playing games?" Grabbing him, he forced him into position on the sink missionary style and pressed his boner firmly against his asshole. "I'll fucking do it! I'll FUCK your ass!" "Don't," Ash protested sliding off. He turned him around and bent him over. Examining his ass, he continued. "It ain't red or anything. I don't see no bruises." Turning to him face on, Ashton met his eyes with a stern expression. "Believe me. He fucked me over good." "Hahaha! Fuck, dude! Someone finally pops your ass cherry, and you're pissed off at him!" "I didn't give him the fucking satisfaction!"

4

THE DEED

Laying bare ass naked on his patio bed, near the swimming pool, with steam rising from the water's surface like phantoms ascending from their graves, Athenas basked in the golden rays of the sun filtering in through the windows of the glass encloser sun bathing while deep in meditation. Pondering on Ashton, and his roots, he felt himself sink deep into the past. It was not long before he found himself surrounded by ruins.

He stood in the midst of the decimated city. Flames ate away at buildings like a cancer, others had been reduced to piles of rubble, trees were stripped bare and set ablaze. Lifeless bodies surrounded him bloody and mutilated. Taking in the gruesome scene, he noticed a figure ascending the hill before him. When close enough for recognition, Pete groaned and straightened as the man settled in front of him. He beheld him covered in ash, blood and deep wounds.

"Griffon," Pete growled. "Athenas! You cold hearted murdering son of a bitch! What interest do you have in MY son?" "I have no interest in 'your son,' Griffon. He's nothing but a fucking weak ass pussy!" "NEVER mistaken his kindhearted nature for weakness!" "He's a fucking old man with an obvious hard on for me!" "Don't you touch him!" "Who the fuck would want to?" "His destiny is not with you, Athenas. Leave him alone." "I'll do as I fucking damn well please, Griffon!" "Leave him alone," Griffon warned.

Redirecting his thoughts, Pete searched for the old man. "Where is Ashton now," he asked himself. A portal opened up in his mind connecting him to the scene. He beheld Ashton standing naked in his bedroom at his open dresser and watched as he drew a pair of clean boxer briefs from the drawer and close it.

Settling bare ass naked behind him, Stone wrapped his arms around his abs, pressed their bodies together and pressed his huge boner into his ass crack. "Stop," Ash protested, pulling away. "Why are you fighting me?" "Why are YOU trying to fuck me?" Taking him into his arms and pressing their lips together, he spoke softly. "Cause you fucking turn me on..... and I'm feeling horny!" "Jerk off then!" Lifting Ashton's leg, he pushed his tip into his hole. "OH! Man," Ash responded. "Why use my hand when I can have you?" Feeling Stone ease his huge boner into him, he called out in ecstasy. "Ho-oooooh!" "Mmmm! Yeahhhh! Your ass is SO tight," Jade observed. "Aww! Aww, Stone! Dude!" Stone proceeded to pound his ass missionary style. "Hahaha! Like I said," Pete sneered," he's nothing but a weak ass old pussy!" Losing interest, Pete ended the link.

Having taken him to unimaginable heights, and filling him with his cum, Stone withdrew his huge boner and laid beside him. Ashton turned onto his side, revealing his sexy ass to the wall. Placing his hand on Jade's hairy pec, he gazed deep into his eyes. "Can I ask you something," he asked. "Sure." He sat up with his legs folded like a pretzel and faced him. Having paused in deep thought he proceeded. "If I didn't look like this, would you have made love to me?" "Yes." "Honestly?" "Honestly." Stone raised up on his elbow and touched his face. "I love you, Ash. I always have. I guess I was just too much of a homophobe to admit it." Taking him by the back of the neck he kissed him passionately.

Hearing the hard rock music play on his phone alerting him of a call, Jade saw that Shamay was calling. Releasing Ashton, he answered. "Hey baby," Stone said cheerfully. "Where are you," Shamay demanded. "What do you mean?" "You're fifteen minutes late, Henderson's pissed!" Spotting the time on the clock, he drew a deep breath. "Shit! I'll be there as soon as I can baby," Jade promised. "You better be, cause I ain't gonna keep covering for your lazy ass," Shamay warned. Ashton watched Stone step into his boxer briefs. "I'm sorry, I gotta go babe. Henderson's gonna have my ass If I don't get to work," Stone told Ash.

While Jade proceeded to dress, the sound of someone at the door filled the air. Answering, Ash discovered Marc leaning against the wall waiting for him to answer. Straightening, he held his upward gaze. "I was beginning to wonder if you were home, Marc announced. Stepping to the side, Ashton allowed him to enter. "How are you doing," Marc asked while Ash shut the door. "I'm alright," Ashton replied as he peered up at Stone who emerged from the bedroom. Jade proceeded to Ashton's side and wrapped his arm around his waist. "Hi," Stone said. "Hey," Marc replied. Turning his attention to his lover, Stone gave Ash a kiss on the cheek. "I gotta go, babe. See you when I get home." "Ok," Ashton said. "I'll call you at lunch," Jade continued. Placing his mouth to his ear and spoking softly, Stone added, "We can jerk off together, baby. Hahaha." He nibbled Ashton's lobe then met Marc's eyes. "Pleasure to meet you," Stone told him. "Likewise," Marc responded.

"He's a good-looking young man. When did you two start fucking," Marc questioned. Ashton gave him a dumb founded look. "Don't look so surprised, babe. The way you two carry on its obvious." "Can I get you something to drink," Ash asked trying to change the subject. "No. But you CAN bend over that table there so I can fuck you." "Excuse me," Ashton inquired. Marc grabbed him and commenced to nestle his neck and lips. Ashton felt his desire for him burst into flame and begin to rage out of control. "I've been wanting to do this since I saw you in the head!" Forcing his tongue into Ashton's mouth, Marc stole a kiss from him. Overwhelmed by the sudden attack of emotions, Ash relented and accepted his kiss. Suddenly, Marc was shirtless and rubbing his chest and belly hair against Ashton's hairless upper body. "Ooooh! Ooooh, Marc," Ashton moaned in ecstasy. Kissing his mouth, and face, Marc gently spoke into his ear. "Undo my belt, and pull my pants down baby."

Coming to his senses, Ash gasped. Marc licked and showered his neck with kisses. "I can't....I can't do this, Marc." Within the beat of a heart, they were naked and Marc was on top of him. His huge, long boner pressed against Ashton's anus. "I'm not asking, Ashton! I WILL fuck your ass!" Cringing and doubling in half from the feel of Marc slowly forcing his huge dick deep into him, he cried out. "Ooooh!" "Mmm," Marc moaned, "Feels good. Doesn't it, babe?" "Marc...." "Aw! You're so tight, baby!" "I can't... I can't do this," Ashton protested weakly. "I'm not taking no for an answer, Ashton," Marc told him, "This IS gonna happen."

Weakening fast to his forceful dominating affections, Ashton commenced to pant and breathe heavily from the sheer movement of his massive cock sliding back and forth within his body. "N-no, Marc... I can't.... I can't.... please," Ash said. With an unexpected burst of telekinesis, Ashton shoved him away. Marc flew backwards and sailed acrost the room and slammed into the wall. Striking his head upon impact, he slumped over as if dead. "OMG! Marc," Ash exclaimed.

Having rushed up to him, Ash took Marc's head lovingly into his hands, then hugged him. "Marc! Marc," Ashton called out to him desperately trying to revive him. Taking his shoulders, he shook him. "Hey. Hey, Marc. Please," Ash continued with tears filling his eyes. With a huge smile suddenly adorning his face, Marc suddenly burst into action and grabbed him with a loud roar. Ashton shrieked in terror. "Hahaha," Marc laughed as he attacked him and forced him into missionary position.

Ashton then cried out and doubled over cringing from the sensation of Marc's huge boner sliding deeper and deeper into his body, panting and gasping at its size. "Hu-uuuuuuuuh! Nnnno, Marc! Ha! Man," Ash cried out straining by its size. Pressing their faces together, Marc spoke gently into his ear," It's alright, baby. It's alright. Relax for me, lover. Relax," Marc soothed. "I can't! I can't," Ash gasped. "Listen to me baby," Marc said, "You don't belong to him. You belong to me." Feeling him move his huge boner inside him, Ashton cringed, the pleasure was overwhelming. "We're gonna take this nice and slow now," Marc said softly in Ashton's ear. "OMG, Marc! It's too big!" "shhhhh," Marc said followed by a tender kiss to Ashton's cheek, "You're alright baby, you're alright. Mmm. You feel good lover."

The sensation was double that he'd felt with any other man. Before long, Ashton was overwhelmed by the sensations ravaging his body causing him to forget he had a boyfriend and he surrendered to Marc's affections. All he could process is how good Marc's making love to him felt and that it was unbelievably strong. He made love to him for twenty long minutes before the sensation neared its apex. Pounding his ass wild, and hard, they both moaned and panted long and loud. The slapping of flesh filled the room and echoed in the hall. Marc kept going as he shot his cum into him, but among the ejaculates, an egg was fired into him. With the deed done, Marc kissed Ashton passionately and panted with him while their bodies slowly relaxed.

Calling out while Marc withdrew his huge cock from within him, Ashton peered up at his phone on the dresser ahead of him. Raising on his knees, with his six inch boner at full mast, he retrieved it from its resting place. Accepting the video call, Pete came on screen. He smiled in his usual devilish manner. "Hey, sexy. How's it going," Athenas asked. "I'm alright," Ash replied. "I have good news, baby. I had someone quit on me just now and I need to fill his spot right away." "I don't have any experience," Ashton reminded him. "Hahaha. Oh, I'll give you plenty of experience, babe. How soon can you get here," Pete asked. "What's the job?" "Go-go boy." "You at the bar," Ashton questioned. "Yeah." "I'll meet you there as soon as I can."

"Hurry the fuck up," Pete added," I need your ass to start today. ""I'll be there when I can," Ash promised. While the screen switched to his cover page, Marc stared into his eyes trying to make sense of his jumbled thoughts. "You really think you can trust him," Marc asked. "I don't know. I don't really know I can trust you. I just cheated on my boyfriend with you, and I don't know what I'm going to tell him."

"You're not meant for him, Ashton. You're mine." "What makes you think that? Because you stuck your dick in me and did the nasty?" "No. Because we share the same blood line." Sliding off the bed, Ash stepped into his briefs. Having pulled them up, he peered over at him. "You're Latino. Aren't you," Ashton asked. "Yes." "Then how is that even possible," Ash questioned him in disbelief.." "Have you heard of Griffon Philips?" "No." "He's an ancestor of yours, lived in Mexico City New Mexico before it became what it is today," Marc began CHAPTER FIVE:

5

VENGENCE

Climbing the hill with the ruins of the decimated city behind him, Griffon fell to his knees, dirty, bloody and drained of energy. Dressed in nothing more than his shredded trousers, his uncut, eight inch dick hung through a hole in his crotch. His sexy ass could be seen as he walked, through the gaping hole in back. He was older, but considered to be still in his prime, forty two.

Standing at six feet, he was still desirable with a rugged appeal. His shoulder length light blonde hair was pulled back in a pony tail. A well-trimmed beard lined his handsome face, he tried to stuff his cock back into his pants, bur it kept falling out. His muscular athletic body was the desire of all who saw him and the result of working the land. Peering ahead, he saw a house and prayed within himself, that the master would answer, or at least another man to avoid the embarrassment of his equipment's exposure.

Having drudged the long distance across the grassy field, he stood at the door and knocked. After a while a tall black man answered. "Yes'ir," he asked," Can I heps ya?" "Might your master be at home?" "I'm sorry sir. He's in the wash." "Who is it, Johnson," a man's voice came from within. "A gentleman be calling." With the sound of water splashing and footsteps of bare feet across a wooden floor, the master of the house appeared at the door. "It's alright Johnson. I'll take it from here." "Yes'ir." Hawkins glanced down at Philip's hand covering his dick, then met his eyes. Griffon glanced at his cut six incher hanging down between his legs, then met his eyes. "After noon, sir. What can I do for you," Hawkins asked.

"I was hoping you might be able to assist me," Griffon announced. "In what way?" "I need someone to tend my wounds." "You are welcome to join me in bath," he invited, "Anna will tend to your sores." "I am not fit to be in the company of a woman, sir," Griffon said timidly. "Anna has several brothers and is studying medicine. I doubt you have anything she has not seen before," Hawkins informed him. "It would not be proper, sir," Griff insisted. "Yes. I know, but she's all I have now and all my boys are at work. Anna! Come down here darling!"

"I believe you know 'Anna' as Mama Hawkins," Marc revealed. "Yes. She died when I was still just a boy." "Griffon married Anna. But she had a child by another man, a Mexican ravaged her, called the boy's name Marco. I was turned by a man, centuries older than myself," Marc lied. "You're a vampire?" "Yes. Ashton." "So... You just want my blood," Ash summized. "No. Something of greater value than that." "What?" "You. Your body, your love…. Your baby. I want you to be my wife." "I gotta get going." Taking him into his arms, Marc nestled his neck and face. "You belong to ME, Ashton!" Ash pulled away and left.

The walk to the lounge seemed longer than usual. Maybe it was the cold of night, maybe it was that for some reason, he was feeling tired, he didn't know. He felt a little uncertain about entering the bar again, but he needed the job, and had no other offers. Pausing at the counter, he noticed the usual company was there in haunt perched at their common places. Pete was wearing a black thong and matching shoes and socks. Ashton peered at his sexy shaped, firm ass. Ash swallowed as he looked away.

Giving him an almost stern, steady gaze, Athenas approached him, circled the counter and settled at his side. "Ashton," he called out with a smile. He took his wrist and kissed his cheek tenderly. "Glad you could make it," he continued, "This way." He led him to the office. "Have a seat," he invited. Pete sat on the edge of the desk across from him while Ash sat in the seat nearby. "How have you been, my friend," Athenas asked. "I've been alright." "That's good. That's good. I've been thinking, Ash. I wanna do something to draw a bigger crowd to the bar. So, I've decided to hire go-go dancers. Naturally, you were one of the first I thought of." "I appreciate it, Mr. Hernandez…" "Pete," he interrupted. "Pete, but I don't have any experience dancing or formal training." "Don't worry about it. Raul has been dancing for years, he'll teach you what you need to know."

"Will I be required to entertain the customers, sexually," asked with worry. "Yes. That would be a given. Don't you think?" Ash sighed. "You okay with that," Pete asked. "I don't know," Ashton said thoughtfully then met his eyes," You really think the customers will want me like that?" "oh, I guarantee it. I need you to do something for me right now,"

Athenas announced. "What is that?" "Strip naked." "Why," Ash inquired with suspicion, then watched him dig through a box at the side that seemed to appear out of nowhere, he held up a packaged black thong. "What size briefs do you wear," Pete asked. "Small." "Try this on. Let's see how it fits."

Ash removed his shirt, then proceeded to slip his shoes off. Observing Ash opening his pants and pulling them down, Pete stroked at his huge cock bulging in his thong. Ash pulled his legs out of his pants and slipped his briefs down to midthigh when he noticed Pete take his boner out and commence to stroke it. "Pete.....Why...." Before Ashton could finish his thought, Athenas took him into his arms and nestled his face and neck. "I'm gonna fuck your ass till you beg for mercy!" "I have a boyfriend now, Pete. I can't." "You think that'll stop me? I don't give a shit about that," Pete told him. Placing his hand on Ashton's abs he stroked them then dropped his hand suddenly. Surprised, Pete drew back and held his gaze. "You're with child!" Ashton laughed. "That's impossible," was his response.

Pete immediately dug his fingers into Ash's pore and proceeded to pull the fetus out. Ashton cried out in pain as blood ran down his belly. With contempt brewing in his eyes, Athenas pierced the embrio with his claws and tossed it into the trash. Ashton stood there stunned and aghast. His mind was a torrent of questions.

Bending on a knee, Pete commenced to lick his abs and cleanse the blood from his body. He slowly made his way to his neck, and kissed him passionately both of them moaning with pleasure. With both their cocks stiff and standing on end, he caressed Ashton's thigh and ass, lifting him onto the desk, he forced his legs back. Ashton blended his voice with his and let out a long moan as Pete slowly penetrated his body with his huge boner and commenced to fuck his ass. "Oh. Oh," Ash moaned. Taking Athenas by the back of his strong shoulders, he held on and watched his sexy ass move as he fucked him. "I can't do this," Ashton told him.

The irresistible aroma of his blood was driving Pete to insanity. He wanted to take Ash to incredible heights before feasting, but the lust for his essence was fast becoming more than he could withstand. Feeling the prick of his fangs, Ashton called out, and succumbed to the pleasures of the flesh as he continued to fuck his ass. With his blood being drained dangerously low, He released an ungodly moan.

His body and face began to dry out and shrivel. Marc appeared with rage filling his expressions. "Get away from him, you fucking son of a bitch," he roared. Shoving him off Ashton, he took Ash into his arms and vanished with him in hand. Ashton was limp and unconscious from the loss of blood and fluid. Appearing with him in his nest, he swept the center piece and condoms, spent and unused off the table in front of the couch and laid his beloved down as the guys of his coven gathered around.

The nest was decorated like any other house commonly inhabited by gay men of youth, but took on a hint of the gothic. Figurines of handsome young men engaging in various sexual acts of homosexuality adorned the lamp tables and coffee table, and along the mantle of the fireplace. Portraits of the clan members hung from the wall along the double wide staircase to the bedrooms upstairs. Candles set in their ornate holders along the walls, on stands around the couch, and strategically placed throughout the room and house were for romantic alure, more than necessity.

The walls had been painted ash white and the framing dark brown. The throw pillows and wood framed couch matched the tables. A portrait of Griffon with his wife Anna hung over the mantle. He was shirtless and visibly naked, She was wearing a slinky black evening gown with a low cut blouse, revealing her voluptuous boobs.

Straddling his body Marc took Ashton into his arms, forced his mouth open and allowed his saliva to drip. "Swallow it baby," He said, tenderly, "Swallow, my love." With the dehydration slowly ebbing away, Ash regained consciousness, stirred and swallowed. "That's it, baby. That's it." Ash panted as he came to. "No! Pete!" "It's alright. It's okay, baby." He said brushing his bangs back," You're okay. You're safe now, my love." Sitting up, Ashton took in the ambiance of his surroundings, then met Marc's eyes. "Where am I?" "You're home, amante." "You're nest," Ash asked. "That's right. How are you feeling?" "I'm alright." "You wanna make love," Marc asked while stroking Ashton's arm. Ash peered at the guys standing at his side. "Do they have to watch," he asked. "They'll get their turn," Marc informed him. Rising to his feet Ashton glanced around. "You looking for something," Marc inquired. With rage dominating his expressions, Ash looked Marc in the eye. "Where are my clothes," he demanded. "What's the matter," Marc asked. "I'm not a fucking whore, Marc! I don't spread my legs for just anyone!" "I never said you did," Marc told him calmly.

Taking him into his arms, Marc kissed him with deep passion. Ash pulled away and headed for the door. Presagio cut him off by leaning between its frame. "Excuse me,"

Ashton said. "Where you going, pussy?" "Let-em go Pres," Marc ordered, "if that's what he really wants," Presagio said, then ran his fingers along Ashton's jawbone tenderly, "But I think he wants it." Unzipping his fly, Pres pulled his cut twelve incher out and slapped it against Ashton's bare abs. "You like that, baby? Yeah? Ya want it? Touch it lover." "That's enough, Presagio! Just let him go," Marc commanded.

Presagio stood at six foot six, had a hairy athletic body with huge pecs and washboard abs. His dark hair cascaded to his shoulders. Sideburns edged his model like handsome face. His Heman shaped torso tapered to small hips, and he had a small, firmed sexy ass. His cock stood full mast at eighteen inches and hung at twelve.

The third and final guy stepped up, his huge, cut cock stiff and at full mast. "'Sup, baby? I'm Broden, Broden McAllen." Peering at his fourteen inch long boner, Ash peered over at Marc who stood nearby stroking his boner. "Marc," Ash whimpered. "It's alright, baby. He won't hurt you," Marc assured him. "No baby," Broden said, "You're gonna like this."

Broden stood at six feet six inches. His light blonde hair flowed like the waves of the sea to his shoulders. Sideburns edged his stunningly handsome face and a soul patch added class to his look. His, Greek god of a body with a tapering torso, hairy large pecs and six pack abs tantalized Ashton. His huge, cut cock hung limp at nine inches and his sexy small, firmed ass was irresistible. Shoving Presagio out of the way, Ashton opened the door and exited the house.

Ashton's eyes grew heavy and watched as Presagio dropped a needle in the trash. Blacking out, Ash fell and Press caught him as he fell. Laying in a dark world of dim light and ominous shadows Ashton woke to an eerie black mist billowing into a cloud at the door to the bedroom they had put him in. The vapor slowly plummeted towards the ground and revealed a figure inside. Pete opened his eyes and stared at him seductively. His glowing red eyes pierced the blackened room and sent chills down Ashton's spine. Stepping from the black cloud, with nothing covering his nakedness, he settled at his side. Raising his hand he raised him off the bed. Ashton began breathing heavily and panted in fear. As he rose into the air his abdomen glowed bright, the fetus could be seen within. In a sudden bright flash of light, Ashton and Pete were gone.

Finding himself on a bolder at the beach, surrounded by the clan, Ash discovered that they were all naked. Athenas ran his claw down Ashton's body to his hips. "Looks like you've been playing the slut with the guys in Marc's clan," Pete observed. Caressing his groin, he took ahold of his boner and proceeded to stroke it. "Gonna have to do something about that, Ashton. Can't have their seed mingle with ours." "Please, Pete. Don't." "Hahaha. What do you think we're going to do?"

He laid his head down while answering. "I don't know," he said then swallowed nervously. Hovering over him, Pete looked Ashton in the eye. "You're right," Athenas said softly in his ear, "We ARE gonna fuck your ass. But I have to get rid of a few things before we do." With the sharp pain of his claw slicing him open from hip to hip, Ash cringed and cried out. Pete dug into his body and pulled the first baby from his body, snapped its neck and tossed it to the side.

Sensing Ashton's pain, Marc entered his room and found that Ash was gone. His eyes glowed a deep red as he realized who'd taken him. "Athenas," Marc said in a deep echoing voice. He instantly connected with his lover. Finding himself the invisible observer, he watched Pete's murderous deeds. Enraged he sent a distress call to his clansmen and all their allies. By the time Marc could respond, Pete had abstracted all but one baby from Ashtons body. Flying through the air, Marc tackled Pete to the ground, pinned him down and commenced to beat his face.

"You fucking son of a bitch," Marc yelled as he proceeded to beat him mercilessly. Responding to Marc's distress call, twelve guys appeared. Seeing, Ashton laying in his blood, cut wide open, and the lifeless babies laying on the floor like discarded bits of trash, rage flooded their emotions, and they attacked the clansmen standing by watching. While Athenas set out to finish the job, Carlos Reyes, Pete's clansman grabbed Marc by the shoulder and thrust his hand into his side. Slashing his opponent's face, blood gushed out and instantly ran down his neck and body.

When the bloody battle had ended Marc's allies laid dead on the ground at the end, Pete's coven retaliated to fight another day. Going up to his lovers masticated body, Marc found Ashton dead from the loss of blood. Marc's clan settled at his side, bloody and cut up from the fight. Griffon and Anna settled behind Marc and peered down at their son. Feeling Marc's pain, Presagio placed his hand on his shoulder. "You can bring him back," he reminded. Turning to him with tears rolling down his face, Marc peered into his eyes. "He's killed them. And all our babies. This is the second time now, Press, The second time!" "Now he's killed Ashton," Broden added," I say we go over there and blow that motherfuckers nest to dust!" "Whose baby is still in him," Anna asked. "Mine," Marc answered. "Is he still alive,' Broden inquired. "I... I.. don't know," Marc muttered. Placing his hand on Marc's shoulder Broden attempted to comfort him. "We can bring him back and start again," Brode soothed. "It doesn't matter what we do or don't do B. We could bring him back till hell freezes over and start over countless times. As long as those assholes are breathing, they'll keep doing this. And before long they'll succeed in killing him for good."

"Have you thought of turning him, as you turned us," Griffon asked. "I'm afraid he'd lose that sweet nature of his if I did," Marc told him. "I say we go and show those motherfuckers who they're fucking with!" "Broden's right. We can't let them get away with this," Presagio agreed.

Marc touched the babe still inside, Ashton's body, and restarted his heart. Holding his hand above his abdomen, the wound closed as the flesh fused together, and healed without a trace. With a snap of his fingers, Ashton vanished, and reappeared, in Marc's bed. "From now on Ashton is not to be left alone. The two of you will alternate shifts watching him." Marc waved his hand and the lifeless mutilated bodies vanished. The allies had abandoned the fight long ago and retreated to the safety of their nests.

That evening, while the last light of twilight ebbed to an end, as if snuffed out like a flame, and darkness ruled once again, Broden rejoined Marc and Presagio's side as they stood across the street from Pete's establishment. Presagio crossed the road and settled at Marc's side. "They're all inside," Press informed. With a stern expression radiating from his countenance, Marc slightly lowered his head. A wave of energy shot out from his brow, and struck the Black Phallus

Lounge. The building exploded in a huge plume of fire and debris that commenced to shower down around them like rain. The entire west half of the building had been cremated. As dust and rubble fell, Pete and his guests stood stunned. Marc sent a telekinetic wave and slammed the door, sealing them inside. "This is for Ashton, you cold hearted, son of a bitch," Marc roared. Focusing on the generator, Marc stuck it with a second wave. Watching the building explode into dust and debris they watched the entire place explode into a cataclysmic fireball.

While the moonlight cut through the blackness of the dark of night and sliced through the window glass of Marc's bedroom, it transformed him and his lover's naked bodies into erotic figures comparable to the sculptures of ancient Rome. Pete and his clan gathered outside Marc's bedroom window. In a heartbeat, a wave of telekinetic energy shot forth from Athenas' hand, and struck the gas line. The house exploded into flames. Presagio ran down the blazing hall with blisters forming on his naked body, a flaming beam fell on him crushing him. Broden, picked Ashton up, and with Marc at his side, carried him to the window, but before they could get it open, Pete struck them with another wave and blew the whole side of the house out.

Setting his attention on the gas main, Pete smiled and laughed devilishly. "Kiss your asses goodbye, motherfuckers," he said. In a flash, the gas main exploded and reduced the house to dust and rubble. "So long assholes," Pete snarled. Having fulfilled his designs, Pete and his clan vanished, and returned to their nest.

Once the dust and ash had settled, and the flames burned themselves out, Marc and his clan emerged from the ruins, dirty, cut up, battered and blistered. As their bodies healed, they searched for their beloved. It was then Broden spotted a bloody, hand stripped of all flesh sticking out from the rubble. "Oh my god," Marc gasped. Alerted to the grizzly remains, the clan went over and unburied Ashton's lifeless body. "NO," Marc shouted. Scooping him up into his arms, he rocked him back and forth with tears streaming down his face. Seething with anger, Broden clenched his fists repeatedly like the beating of a heart. Presagio placed his hands on his friend's shoulder. "He's too far gone, Pres," Marc said while peering back at him," I can't bring him back this time. They're both gone." Striking a tree with his fist, Broden yelled. "That son of a bitch!" Brode turned to Marc and glared into his eyes.

"That asshole has crossed the fucking line this time! I say we go in there and rip their fucking balls off," Broden roared. "What good would that do, Brod," Marc asked," Ashton would still be gone." "So we let them get away with this and do NOTHING," Broden asked in rage. With agony eating away at his heart, Marc ran his fingers through the back of Ashton's hair and cringed at the loss. "Go-o-o-od! Baby, why'd they do this?" "What do you wanna do, Marc," Presagio asked. "Are we gonna just let them get away with this," Broden demanded to know. Marc peered up into his rage filled eyes. "You really think vengeance will make any difference, Broden? Ashton's GONE! He's DEAD! Noone can bring him back!"

THE END

Printed in the United States
by Baker & Taylor Publisher Services